TJ TRAPPER
BULLY ZAPPER

ZAP

TJ Zaps the Freeze Out
Stopping the Silent Treatment

CHATTER

CHATTER

hrumpff

magic wagon

BOOK 3

written by
Lisa Mullarkey

illustrated by
Gary LaCoste

visit us at www.abdopublishing.com

To my sixth grade teacher- the real Ms. Morris. —LM
For Ashley —GL

Published by Magic Wagon, a division of the ABDO Group,
PO Box 398166, Minneapolis, MN 55439. Copyright © 2013 by
Abdo Consulting Group, Inc. International copyrights reserved
in all countries. All rights reserved. No part of this book may
be reproduced in any form without written permission from the
publisher.

Calico Chapter Books™ is a trademark and logo of Magic Wagon.

Printed in the United States of America, North Mankato, Minnesota.
052012
092012
This book contains at least 10% recycled materials.

Text by Lisa Mullarkey
Illustrations by Gary LaCoste
Edited by Stephanie Hedlund and Rochelle Baltzer
Cover and interior design by Neil Klinepier

Library of Congress Cataloging-in-Publication Data
Mullarkey, Lisa.
  TJ zaps the freeze out : stopping the silent treatment / by Lisa
Mullarkey ; illustrated by Gary LaCoste.
     p. cm. -- (TJ Trapper, bully zapper ; bk. 3)
  Summary: When Livvy chooses a goldfish as the class pet, some
of the other children decide to freeze her out, and TJ has to choose
between his friend and being frozen out himself--or find a way to
make them see that their bullying behavior is wrong.
  ISBN 978-1-61641-907-3
  1. Bullying--Juvenile fiction. 2. Friendship--Juvenile fiction. 3.
Schools--Juvenile fiction. 4. Goldfish--Juvenile fiction. [1. Bullies-
-Fiction. 2. Friendship--Fiction. 3. Schools--Fiction. 4. Goldfish--
Fiction. 5. Behavior--Fiction.] I. LaCoste, Gary, ill. II. Title.
  PZ7.M91148Tjf 2012
  813.6--dc23   2012008065

Contents

Lowlife Guppies

Today should have been called Livvy Armstrong Day.

Livvy was "Star of the Day." That meant she got to read a book to the kindergartners and eat lunch with Ms. Perry.

She also won a homework pass for bringing in the most box tops.

Her name was even announced over the loudspeaker for running the fastest mile in gym class.

And at the end of the day, Ms. Perry made a special announcement. "Class, as you know, I didn't want a class pet. But after having lunch with Livvy, I changed my mind."

Everyone cheered.

Ethan and I stared at each other. We'd been bugging Ms. Perry for a pet since the first day of school.

"And since it was her idea," said Ms. Perry, "she's going to surprise us with a pet tomorrow."

Ethan crossed his arms. "*Her* idea?"

I sighed. "At least we'll have a pet."

Livvy bounced over to us. "I'm thinking of getting a goldfish."

"A goldfish!" Ethan shrieked. "No way! *Anything* but a goldfish!"

"We *always* have goldfish, Livvy. In first grade, we had Salt and Pepper. In second grade, we had Pip and Pop. Last year, we had Tater and Tot. No one wants a fish."

"Tater was my favorite," said Maxi, moving her finger in a circle. "He'd swim round and round all day long."

"That's the only thing fish can do. They're boring," I said. "The fifth graders are going to call us lowlife guppies."

"*Again*," said Ethan. He slumped down in his chair. His face was red. "If you bring in a fish, I won't talk to you anymore."

Livvy looked surprised. Then mad. "I didn't say I was *definitely* getting a fish. I'm going to Pet Palace tonight. I might get a bearded gecko."

"A gecko would be great," I said. "Ethan has one. It would be way better than a fish."

"Way, way, way better than a goldfish," said Ethan.

"Then a gecko it is," said Livvy. "You can count on me."

But when I saw her drawing goldfish all over her notebook that afternoon, I wasn't so sure. She drew little hearts for their tails.

"What if we get another goldfish?" I asked Ethan after school.

"Trust me," said Ethan. "We're *not* getting another goldfish."

That's when he told me The Plan.

That night, I set my alarm clock for seven o'clock. Dad's clock radio sat on my dresser. It was set to go off at seven fifteen. My old Barney clock was hidden behind my baseball mitt ready to sing, "I Love You" at seven twenty. What can I say? We were desperate.

"I found the travel clock," Auntie Stella said from the doorway. She looked around and shook her head. "I don't think you'll need it."

"You never know." I grabbed the clock and set it for seven thirty. "The power could go out."

She scanned the room one last time. "Night, TJ. I hope it works out for you tomorrow. Are you positive Livvy is getting there at eight?"

Auntie Stella isn't my real aunt. But she's been helping my dad take care of me ever since I was born. Dad always says we can't live without her and she can't live without us. I think he's right. Even though I call her Auntie Stella, everyone thinks she's my grandmother.

I flicked off my lamp. "That's what Ethan said. Mr. Wong is driving us to school early. Before eight. We'll have Ethan's gecko in the car just in case."

"What if she shows up with a fish?" asked Auntie Stella.

"She won't," I said. "A promise is a promise. But in case she does, we'll talk her into bringing the gecko inside instead. Mr. Wong will wait in the car. We'll give the goldfish to him."

"Sounds like a good plan," said Auntie Stella as she kissed my forehead.

And it was.

At six fifty-nine, I woke up and turned off my alarm clock. I jumped out of bed and turned off all the alarms. After getting dressed, I crept down the steps to the kitchen.

"Morning, TJ," Dad yawned as he poured me a glass of juice. "Auntie Stella told me you're hoping to have a gecko for a class pet. I forgot how much you wanted a pet." He stirred his coffee. "Maybe we can stop by Pet Palace this weekend and have a look. Maybe it's time we get a pet."

I wasn't expecting this! My heart pounded. "How about a dog?"

He frowned. "Dogs need lots of exercise. Who wants to get up at six to walk a dog? Not me." He sipped his coffee. "How about something in a cage?"

Before I could say *rabbit*, Auntie Stella spoke up. "Nothing messy. An easy-to-clean cage. I'm busy enough cleaning up after both of you. Cooking for both of you. Washing clothes for both of you. Busy, busy, busy."

There goes that idea.

Dad waved his hand in front of his nose. "Nothing smelly."

Nix the pet skunk I saw on television. My list grew shorter.

Dad slid over a box of doughnuts.

"Something without fur," he said. "Auntie Stella is allergic to most fur."

And shorter and shorter . . .

"Nothing that eats live bugs or critters," said Auntie Stella. "That makes me want to throw up!"

And shrinking some more . . .

Then Dad folded his newspaper and said, "How about a goldfish?"

"A goldfish?" I shook my head. "I'm anti-goldfish! I'm anti- redfish, bluefish, one fish, two fish! I hate fish!" I took a deep breath. "That's what Livvy wants."

Auntie Stella slowly shook her head. "What's your dad thinking, TJ? Want me to snap him with the old dish towel?"

Dad put his arms up in the air. "I didn't know about Livvy and the fish. Sorry!"

Twenty minutes later, Ethan's dad honked the horn. I grabbed my backpack. "Wish me luck!"

"All ready for the big switch-a-roo?" asked Mr. Wong.

I nodded.

"If Livvy doesn't have a gecko," said Ethan, "she can say she brought Spike. She promised it wouldn't be a fish."

"But will she keep her promise?" asked Mr. Wong

"She can't break a promise," I said.

"Or else," whispered Ethan.

"Or else what?" I asked.

"Or else I'll give her the silent treatment."

He meant it, too. Once he stopped

talking to me for a whole day because I bought the last pretzel at lunch.

After his dad parked the car, Ethan and I headed toward the door with Spike. Up ahead, we could see Livvy. She was early! She was talking to someone and pointing to a box on the ground.

"She better be talking to her mom or dad," said Ethan.

But she wasn't.

"TJ! Ethan!" called out Ms. Perry. "Wait until you see what Livvy got for our class pet. It's perfect!"

"Ms. Perry!" I grumbled. "The old switch-a-roo is switch-a-ruined."

"Unless she has a gecko," said Ethan as he ran back to the car with Spike.

I crossed my fingers. This year had to be different. No more guppies. No more disgusting fish flakes.

My stomach growled.

I suddenly had the urge for a tuna fish sandwich.

Meet Morty

After the Pledge of Allegiance, Ms. Perry peeked under the cloth draped over a bowl. She nodded and straightened her skirt. "It really is a wonderful choice!"

Livvy flashed a smile at the class as she trudged over to the science table. "Salutations, class! Today is a special day. Our new class pet will teach us about responsibility. And about being a caring citizen. Thanks to this class, I've learned to be a much better citizen."

"What a suck-up!" Ethan whispered as he kissed the air a few times. "She *better* have a gecko."

Livvy took a deep breath. "It's time for the big reveal."

"I can't look," Ethan groaned as he covered his eyes.

Like a magician, Livvy snatched the sheet off of the bowl.

Everyone gasped.

I groaned.

It was a goldfish! A stinkin' goldfish!

Kids bolted out of their seats and crowded around the fish.

I didn't budge.

Ethan uncovered his eyes. "What happened?" he asked.

"I'll tell you what happened," I mumbled. "We're the lowlife guppies. Again."

A minute later, Ms. Perry announced, "Our goldfish needs a name." She picked up a piece of chalk. "Any ideas?"

"Jaws!" yelled Livvy.

"Tater Tot 2," said Kelli.

Maxi raised her hand. "Goldie?"

"Goldie was the name of the kindergarten fish last year," said Ethan.

Ms. Perry's face brightened. "Go back to your seats and spend the next five minutes brainstorming names. Write your favorite one on a piece of paper. Then I'll pick one."

As Ms. Perry passed out scrap paper, I chewed on my pencil. I wasn't about to waste time thinking up a name for a dumb fish. So I chose a name I knew would never be picked: Morty. It was the name of my dentist. Then I gave the paper to Ms. Perry.

"Do I have everyone's papers?" she asked a minute later. She read a few of the names as she unfolded the papers. "Swimmy, Nemo, Gully, Tangerine, Glimmer, or Nugget . . ."

Livvy clapped each time a name was read.

"Got it!" said Ms. Perry as she held up a slip of paper. "This one jumped out at me because it was my great-grandfather's name."

Livvy interrupted. "The suspense is killing me, Ms. Perry! Tell us!"

Ms. Perry smiled. "Ladies and gentlemen, may I present . . . Morty."

Morty!? Could this day get any worse?

At snack time, I plopped my snack bag on the back table and sat next to Ethan. A minute later, Livvy slid her chair over.

"What kind of name is Morty?" asked Livvy. "Who do you think named him, Ethan?"

He ignored her.

"Well," she said, "I'd be *Morty-fied* if I picked that name."

I changed the subject as I grabbed a chip out of Livvy's bag. "What happened to the gecko? I thought you said we could count on you. You promised us you were getting a gecko. That we'd be goldfish-free."

Livvy shrugged. "What we have is much better than a gecko. Morty isn't *just* a goldfish. He's completely white. That makes him an albino goldfish. They're rare."

Ethan cleared his throat. "TJ, will you tell Livvy that they aren't that rare. My neighbor has two of them." Then he added. "And tell her no one wanted another stupid fish."

"I can hear you, Ethan," said Livvy.

Maxi said, "It's okay with me."

"That's because you have pets at home," I said.

Livvy smirked and tilted her head toward Ethan. "I guess it burns his gills."

Everyone laughed except Ethan and me.

Ms. Perry appeared out of nowhere. "Some of you seem disappointed that we have a goldfish. But keep in mind that we must respect Livvy's choice. I think Morty is darling." When no one said anything, she cleared her voice. "Am I being clear?"

Ethan and I nodded. Then I walked over to the bowl and introduced myself to Morty. I had to at least pretend to like him. If I didn't, Ms. Perry would get mad. Then she'd call Dad.

I'd be a goner. I'd be swimming with the sharks.

FHO
(Freeze Her Out)

"Did your class get the gecko?" asked Auntie Stella when she picked me up from school. She peeked into my classroom. "I've been dying to find out."

"Nope." I swung my backpack onto my shoulders. "Another stupid goldfish," I whispered. "An albino goldfish."

"Is that it?" asked Auntie Stella, pointing to the bowl on the science table. "You know me, kiddo. I want to see it!"

Before I could stop her, she walked into the classroom.

Livvy was still there packing up her backpack and talking to Ms. Perry.

"So, Livvy," said Auntie Stella, "TJ said you picked out an albino goldfish for the class. How exciting!"

Livvy bobbed her head up and down.

"Hello, Stella," said Ms. Perry. "Would you like to see it?"

I rolled my eyes. We'd never get out of here now.

Livvy picked up the bowl. "I'm in charge of taking care of Morty this weekend." She smooshed her face up to the bowl. "But Ms.

Perry said that we're going to take turns fish-sitting him on weekends."

I dropped my backpack. "You picked the goldfish. Shouldn't you take care of it?"

Auntie Stella glared at me. I could tell she wished she had a dish towel on her.

"It's a CLASS pet," said Livvy. "Ms. Perry said we all need to share the responsibility."

"That's right, TJ," said Ms. Perry. "You are a part of this classroom, aren't you? All members of this caring community need to step up and help care for our class pet."

Auntie Stella peered into the bowl. "He really is an albino. I don't see a drop of color on him anywhere."

Ms. Perry looked in, too. "Nope. Me either. That's fascinating. Isn't it, TJ?"

I didn't say a word until Auntie Stella gave me the look again.

"Fascinating," I said. "Morty's the best pet ever." Not.

When I got to the car, Ethan was waiting for me. When his mom started to talk to Auntie Stella, he pulled me behind the car.

"Why were you talking to Livvy?" asked Ethan.

I replied, "Because she was talking to me."

"You need to FHO," he said.

I scratched my head. "What does FHO mean?"

"My sister says it all the time. It means Freeze Her Out. Or Freeze Him Out."

"What does that even mean?" I asked.

"We ignore her. She talks to us, we pretend we don't hear her. We get everyone to do it. She'll feel really bad about getting that stupid fish. Maybe she'll feel so bad she'll take Morty back and get a gecko."

I looked at Auntie Stella to make sure she couldn't hear us. "That doesn't seem right, Ethan."

"What doesn't seem right?" asked Auntie Stella.

She hears everything!

Ethan waved at Auntie Stella. "Nothing. Just talking about a math problem."

Auntie Stella went back to talking to Mrs. Wong while I hopped in the car.

Ethan leaned into the open window. "Think about it," he whispered. "FHO."

On the way home, I didn't think about freezing anyone out. I just thought about having to fish-sit Morty over an entire weekend.

When I got home, I turned Dad's computer on and ran my fingers across the keyboard.

I thought for a minute then went to work typing up the perfect e-mail.

Dear Ms. Perry,

Did you know that Livvy wants to be the official fish-sitter EVERY weekend? Shouldn't you let her? Having me take care of a fish is NOT a good idea. Watching Morty at my house could be hazardous to his health. My Auntie Stella is a vegetarian and eats a lot of fish. What if she filets him? Did you know that my dad is allergic to fish? Morty might be allergic to him, too.

Your student,

TJ Trapper

I pressed send and kicked my feet up on the desk. Now I just had to wait and see if Ms. Perry would take the bait.

Fish Have Feelings, Too!

Livvy wasn't in school on Monday morning. She didn't come to school until after lunch was over. Her eyes were red. She rushed by me and put the fishbowl on the science table.

"Are you okay?" asked Kelli during free reading time.

Livvy nodded. "I had a headache."

I headed over to the bookcase. I stopped at the science table when I heard Maxi talking to Ethan.

"It's not a real albino goldfish," said Maxi. "Look at the blue streak on the tail."

Ethan pressed his nose up to the glass. "I can't see it."

I bent down and squinted. Sure enough, there was a shimmery blue streak on the

tip of Morty's tail. "I see it. Right on the end." I looked at Maxi. "That's weird. It wasn't there the other day."

Livvy marched over and grabbed the bowl. "Yes, it was. Give Morty room. Stop bugging him."

Ethan looked around the room. "Did I hear someone say something?"

Lamar laughed. "I didn't. Must be a pesky fly. Someone should squash it."

Maxi's mouth dropped open. She hissed at Ethan and Lamar, "Be nice." She touched Livvy's arm. "We weren't bugging him. Honest. We were just checking out his tail. Can you see the blue streak on the end of it?"

Livvy ignored Maxi's question. Then she stuck her tongue out at Lamar and Ethan and stormed away with the bowl.

She walked so fast that some of the water splashed out of the bowl.

"I have 20/20 vision with my glasses," said Maxi. "I know I saw a blue streak." Then she took of her glasses. "Maybe I had 20/20 vision. Maybe I need to get stronger glasses." She asked Ms. Perry if she could go to the nurse.

A minute later, Livvy and Ms. Perry hung a chart on the board.

"Boys and girls, we all must take responsibility for Morty," said Ms. Perry. "From now on, we'll be sharing weekend fish-sitting duties. Livvy made a schedule over the weekend. If anyone has a problem with their assigned weekend, please let me know."

As I lined up for gym, I scanned the list. There I was, confirmed fish hater, on top. Just my luck!

"You're second," said Livvy to Ethan.

But Ethan ignored her again. She put her hands on her hips and ran down the list of names. "Look, Kelli. You're after Ethan."

Kelli nodded but didn't say anything. Was Kelli freezing her out, too?

"Lamar's after Kelli," said Livvy. "Have you ever taken care of a pet before?"

Lamar stared straight ahead.

"Be that way," said Livvy as her eyes filled up with tears. "Come on, Maxi," she said. "Let's line up for gym."

During gym class, I noticed that most of the kids weren't talking to Livvy. Maxi was. Kelli did a little. I could tell it upset Livvy.

When I got back from gym, I found a note on my desk:

Dear TJ,

I read your e-mail about leaving all fish-sitting duties to Livvy. That doesn't seem fair, does it? I called Auntie Stella. She assures me she will do her best NOT to eat Morty for breakfast, lunch, or dinner. She also said your father would be delighted to meet Morty.

Sincerely,

Ms. Perry

P.S. She also said to tell you that the dish towel was ready. I'm not sure what that means...

I laughed.

Under the note was a folder labeled Fish-Sitting Instructions. Livvy had written down so many directions that they took up two whole pages.

1. Feed Morty two shakes—not three—of fish flakes a day.

2. Sing Morty a song. "Under the Sea" from *The Little Mermaid* is his favorite.

3. Tell Morty a bedtime story. No shark tales!

4. Night-lights are a must. Morty is afraid of the dark.

5. Change the distilled water in the bowl every other day. Scoop Morty up and put him in a temporary bowl while you scrub the grime away. DO NOT USE SOAP. It will kill Morty.

6. When eating breakfast, have Morty join you. Make him feel like part of your family.

7. Bring Morty into the bathroom with you. The sound of running water makes him feel at home.

8. Don't eat fish products when Morty is with you. Fish have feelings, too.

Fish have feelings, too? This was ridiculous. Morty was a fish! Not a person. I reread the instructions. Sing to him? Nightlights? No way! I glanced over at Morty. How hard could it be?

If he survived a weekend with Livvy, he'd survive hanging out with me.

What could go wrong?

Off the Deep End

I didn't give fish-sitting another thought until Friday afternoon.

"Are you ready for Morty this weekend?" asked Livvy. She looked worried. "I'll be away the whole weekend." She pulled a piece of paper out of her pocket. "Here's my mom's cell number in case you need to call me." Then she lowered her voice. "That is if you're still talking to me." She looked over at the other kids.

I grabbed the number. "I'll be okay, Livvy. Promise."

Ethan whispered, "FHO."

"What does FHO mean?" asked Livvy. "I heard that, Ethan."

Ethan whispered it again. "FHO."

Then Lamar looked at me and mouthed, "Or we're going to FYO."

FYO. Freeze You Out.

Great. Just great. But I had more important things to worry about. Like what was I supposed to do with Morty for a whole weekend?

When I got home, I sat at the kitchen table. "Livvy's gone off the deep end," I said, holding up the instructions.

Auntie Stella laughed. "You may not have wanted a fish as a class pet but you are part of the class," she reminded me. "You need to pitch in."

I grabbed a brownie off a plate. "Do I have to follow *all* of the directions?"

"It depends," said Auntie Stella. "Do you want that brownie?"

I pushed my nose up to the glass and shook some fish flakes into the water. "Hey, Morty. Are you as thrilled to be stuck with me as I am with you?"

The flakes reminded me of food. "What's for dinner?"

Auntie Stella opened the freezer. "Macaroni and cheese and fish sticks."

"Fish sticks? Don't tell Livvy! If she knew you mentioned dinner and fish in the same sentence, she'd arrest you for fish abuse."

Auntie Stella looked in the fridge. "How about chicken fingers instead?"

"Fish sticks are fine," I answered. "Morty won't know the difference."

I just had to make sure Livvy didn't find out!

Lying in bed that night, I felt slightly guilty for not following rule number three:

Tell Morty a bedtime story. No shark tales! I hopped out of bed and propped my social studies book near his bowl. Why was I worrying anyway? Morty was just a fish.

The next morning, I brought Morty's bowl to the kitchen table. Staring at Morty, I realized two things: 1. It must be boring swimming around in a bowl all day long and 2. If I had to pay attention to Morty, I might as well make the most of it.

As I poured a bowl of cereal, the prize—a miniature basketball hoop with a net—popped out. The basketball was attached by a string so it wouldn't bounce off the table. A neat prize, if you were three years old. I was about to toss it in the trash when I wondered if Morty would like it. It was just the right size for him.

I ripped the basketball off and plunked the stand and hoop into the bowl. It sunk to the bottom and rested on its side. Not exactly a thrill-a-minute, but better than nothing.

Morty swam up to the net a few times and darted away. "Come on, Morty. You'll like swimming through the net. I'll tell you what, each time you do, you'll earn two points. Once you earn 20, I'll give you a treat."

Ten minutes later, Morty had scored 22 points. "Good job, Morty." I dropped a pinch of dried worms into his bowl. I figured my responsibilities were over for the day.

On Sunday night, I went to my room and started my homework.

Dad came in a few minutes later carrying the fishbowl. He plunked it down on my desk. "How ya doing, buddy? I thought

Morty could use a change of scenery. It's drafty in the kitchen." He sat on my bed.

I thought about Ethan and Lamar. I thought about Livvy, too. "Dad, do you know what FHO means?"

"I hear it used all the time at the high school," he said. "It means freezing someone out. Not talking to them. Excluding them from your group." Then he bit his lip. "How come you know what it means?"

I sighed. "I'd rather not say. But it's happening to someone in our class. And if I don't stop talking to someone, then the kids are going to freeze me out, too."

"Seems like you have a problem, TJ." He rubbed his eyes. "You know that freezing someone out is bully behavior, don't you? It's not right. What are you going to do?"

"Well, I'm not going to stop talking to the person. She didn't really do anything wrong. I mean, she just bought a fish. It's not that big of a deal."

I covered my mouth. Now he knew it was Livvy.

"Has Livvy told anyone?" he asked. "She should tell Ms. Perry or Mrs. Morris. I bet they don't know because the kids are probably smart enough to act like everything is fine when an adult is around."

I nodded. "Yep. They talk to her in front of Ms. Perry."

Dad stood. "I'd suggest you report it to Ms. Perry and tell her before it gets any worse."

"But that would get the kids in trouble," I said. "I don't want anyone to get in trouble or think I'm a tattletale."

Dad narrowed his eyes. "TJ, you know the difference between reporting and tattling. Reporting is to help kids get out of trouble. I know you don't want Livvy to be bullied. You have a choice to make. Do you want to be a bystander or an upstander?"

"Upstander," I said. "I'll tell the kids that it's bullying. Maybe that will work."

"Let me know how it works out, TJ," said Dad as he got up. "I'm here for you if you want to talk again."

After he left, I noticed the scum on the side of Morty's bowl. Not that Morty cared. He was just happy to swim in circles all day long. But I knew Auntie Stella would care. Livvy, too.

"I'll tell you what, Morty, I'm going to clean out your bowl," I told him. Anything to avoid homework.

I brought Morty to the bathroom and put him in a plastic container. I filled his bowl with hot, soapy water and scrubbed it until it sparkled. Twenty minutes later, I refilled the bowl with fresh water and dropped Morty back inside.

"You're lucky you don't have homework, Morty. No essays. No tests.

Maybe fish life has advantages." I sat at my desk and pulled out my homework folder. I had to write a two-page report on my hero.

"Well, Morty, what do you think? Who's your hero? Nemo? Jacques Cousteau?" He swam through the basketball hoop. "Don't want to talk, huh?" I tapped my pencil against the bowl. "Oh, you want to know who *my* hero is? Thanks for asking. Let's see . . ." I rattled off a long list and then wrote my report.

I read it to Morty. He seemed impressed and even blew me a bubble.

Now if I could impress Ms. Perry . . .

De-bullied

"How's Morty?" asked Livvy when I walked into class Monday morning.

"He survived," I said as I slid his bowl onto the science table.

"Did you read him a book?" asked Livvy. "Sing him a song?" She put her hands on her hips. "I hope you didn't eat anything that offended him."

Maxi and Ethan walked over. Ethan didn't look at Livvy.

"He was a good little fish," I said. "He had one time-out, though. He was swimming three miles per hour in a two miles per hour zone."

Ethan and Maxi laughed. Livvy barely cracked a smile.

"Seriously, Livvy. He's fine," I said. "More than fine. Any idiot can take care of a fish."

Livvy puffed her cheeks. "Are you saying I'm an idiot?"

Whoa! Where did she get that? Ms. Perry looked over. "Is there a problem?"

"No problem," I eeked out. "Livvy, I didn't call you an idiot. I just meant that it's pretty easy *not* to mess up while fish-sitting."

Livvy's eyes were glassy. I changed the subject. "Look at the cool toy I put in there.

Morty loves it. Didn't you have a hoop in your fish tank last year, Lamar?"

But Lamar didn't answer me. He looked at Ethan. "Did someone say something?"

Ethan's face turned red. "Sorry, TJ," he whispered as he rushed back to his seat.

The big freeze-out had begun.

I walked over to Ethan and Lamar. "You're both being bullies. Not talking to someone just because you didn't get your way is being a bully."

Then I stared at Ethan. "When Livvy was bullying us, you told her you couldn't be friends with her if she wasn't being nice to your friends. Well, I can't be friends with you if you can't be nice to my friends. Got it?"

Then I sat down at my desk.

No one seemed like they were in a good mood today. Even Morty seemed different. He wasn't swimming as fast as usual. But when I pointed it out to Livvy after lunch, she got mad.

"He's fine, TJ," said Livvy as she walked away. "Mind your own business."

Mind my own business? Ha! I ripped out a piece of paper from my notebook and wrote her a message.

Livvy,

I thought Morty was everyone's business now that we're all helping to take care of him. You need to relax. Morty is just a fish. And if I minded my own business, Lamar and Ethan would be talking to me.

TJ

As I tossed it to her, Ms. Perry made an announcement. "Don't forget that there's no homework tonight due to the Teacher In-service Day tomorrow. I'm sure everyone will enjoy their day off."

Livvy started to freak out. "Who will take care of Morty? He can't stay here alone!" She glanced over at me.

"Don't look at me," I said. "I've already done my fish-sitting."

Ms. Perry agreed. "Good point, Livvy. I can understand your concern. Do you think you can take Morty home today and bring him back on Wednesday morning?"

Livvy nodded.

At dinner that night, I told Dad and Auntie Stella all about Morty's day and how his basketball skills impressed the kids. Well, except for Ethan and Lamar.

Auntie Stella wiped her mouth. "Speaking of basketball, we're driving

Ethan to practice tonight. His dad is dropping him off any minute."

Just then, the doorbell rang. I thought it would be Ethan. But it wasn't. It was Livvy. She was holding her backpack. "I took your folder by mistake when I packed up," she said. Then she sniffed the air. "Do I smell tuna fish?"

Auntie Stella came to the door. "Want some? There's plenty. I made it for lunch tomorrow."

Livvy's mouth dropped open. "Did you forget about rule number eight, TJ?"

Rule eight? She wanted me to memorize all of Morty's rules? I could barely remember my nine timetables math facts.

"Relax, Livvy. My fish-sitting duties are over. Morty's at your house, remember? This is a no-fish zone today."

Auntie Stella patted Livvy on the back. "Morty sure is cute. I bet everyone loves him."

"Not everyone loves him," said Livvy in a voice only I could hear. "Right, TJ?"

That's when Ethan came to the door. He looked surprised to see Livvy.

"Um . . . hi," he stuttered.

Now Livvy ignored him. "Do I hear a fly buzzing around? They are so pesky, aren't they, TJ?" Then she waved good-bye and ran down the steps to her mom's car.

"What's wrong with her?" asked Ethan. "All I did was say hello."

"It's not fun to be frozen out, is it?" I asked.

Ethan looked surprised. "Is she going to freeze me out? Get all the kids to stop talking to me?" He looked upset.

"Would it bother you?" I asked. "I mean, you acted like a bully. If you bully someone, chances are you'll be bullied, too."

He took a deep breath. "Okay, TJ, I get it. I was wrong. I really didn't think I was acting like a bully. And you're right.

I would hate it if someone did that to me. I'm sorry."

"Don't tell me you're sorry," I said. "Tell Livvy."

Then I zapped his arm. "You've just been de-bullied. Thanks to me, TJ Trapper, Bully Zapper."

Morty, the Jewish Fish

At ten thirty the next day, the phone rang. A few minutes later, Auntie Stella came into my room. "That was Mrs. Armstrong. She wants us to go over there for dinner tonight to thank us for helping Livvy adjust to school."

"Really?" I tossed my comic book on the floor. "I have to eat at a girl's house?"

Auntie Stella frowned. "The Armstrongs live 3,000 miles from their nearest relatives. I think Livvy's lonely." Then she looked me in the eye. "You're going." She shook a dish towel. "Or else."

At five o'clock, Auntie Stella, Dad, and I knocked on Livvy's door.

We weren't inside for more than two minutes before Livvy told me about her phone call from Ethan.

"He apologized and said he feels awful," said Livvy. "He was just having a bad week. He said that you were really mad at him. You stuck up for me. Thanks!"

"What did you say?" I asked.

"I remembered how I acted when I first came to school. Ethan was really nice to me. So, I told him that we all have bad days. Even weeks. That's what Mrs.

Morris says to me all the time when I meet with her. I'm working on not taking out my bad days on my friends and family. I guess Ethan is, too."

Then she showed me a picture she took of Morty that was hanging on the refrigerator.

"Did you ever see such a cute fish?" she asked.

"They all look the same to me," I said.

She bit her lip. "Well, Morty looks different to me. And he's Jewish. Just like me."

"A Jewish fish?" I asked. "I didn't know they had a religion." Then I lifted Morty's bowl so I could get a better look at him. "Well, he's a lucky fish. He'll get eight days of presents for Hanukkah. Pretty cool deal, don't you think, Morty?"

Livvy laughed. "But you get a holiday that lets you gnaw ears off of chocolate bunnies at five o'clock in the morning. And you get to stuff your mouth with jelly beans and marshmallow chicks until your teeth hurt."

She was right! "But the Easter Bunny doesn't come eight days in a row," I said. "Why do you celebrate Hanukkah for eight days anyway?"

For the next twenty minutes, Livvy filled us in on the Festival of Lights and I taught her the real story of Easter.

"What's your favorite holiday tradition, TJ?" asked Mrs. Armstrong at dinner.

"Making cookies," I said. "Last year we spent six hours baking them for Christmas. We give them out to everyone. My teachers, the mail carrier, our neighbors and friends. We also make Easter egg cookies, but we don't share those. We only make a batch." Then I had an idea. "Maybe when Christmas comes, we can make cookies together."

Livvy looked surprised. "Really?"

"Just don't ask me to make any for Morty," I said.

Livvy giggled and shifted in her seat. "My favorite Hanukkah tradition is when Poppy lights the menorah on the first night and tells the story of Hanukkah. After we say prayers, Grammy hides chocolate coins. Then we have to look for them. I found twenty-seven coins last year."

Then she rubbed her eyes. "I know it sounds crazy, but Poppy would drag the tents out of the attic and our whole family would sleep outside on the first and last nights of Hanukkah. We'd make s'mores

and tell stories around the campfire, too."
Livvy wiped her mouth and excused
herself from the table.

Mrs. Armstrong followed her into the
other room.

"I think Livvy's upset that this will
be her first Hanukkah without Poppy

and Grammy," said Mr. Armstrong. "It's too expensive to fly home this year." He sighed. "And they don't want to travel so far at their age." He pushed his plate away. "It can be lonely when your nearest family is 3,000 miles away."

"It's still over a month away," I said. "Maybe you'll have enough money saved by then."

Now Mr. Armstrong looked sad. "I know this may sound odd, but I think that's why Livvy loves Morty so much. Morty reminds her of home. Her Poppy gave her tropical fish for Hanukkah last year before we knew we were moving. When we moved here, she had to leave them behind. Poppy's keeping an eye on them for us."

No wonder Morty meant so much to Livvy. Now I felt awful!

Livvy's eyes were red when she came back in for dessert. Everyone looked gloomy. I had to think of something fast.

"Let's get Morty," I suggested. "He should be here for dessert. He's family, isn't he?"

Livvy's eyes lit up. "Really? Do you think so? He's in my room. I'll get him."

We didn't leave until ten o'clock that night. We were having too much fun.

When I left, I turned back and shouted, "Hey, Livvy, why are fish so smart?"

Livvy gave me two thumbs-up. "Because they live in schools!"

Fish Pox

Livvy was late to school again the next day. "Is everything okay?" asked Ms. Perry as she glanced at the clock.

Livvy nodded and brought Morty over to the science center. I tried to get her attention but she wouldn't look at me. Or Maxi. Or anyone else.

During snack, I pushed my chair over to her table. "What's wrong, Livvy?"

"I have another headache. I'm okay."

Maxi carried Morty over to us. "What's she so upset about?" she whispered.

I pretended I didn't know, but I had a hunch she missed Poppy. Big time.

I peered into the bowl. "Morty might not be feeling too well either. It looks like he has a case of the chicken pox. Didn't Maxi's cousin have them last week?"

Maxi nodded and scratched her arm. "I get itchy thinking about it." She held the bowl up to the light. "Fish can't catch chicken pox."

"Are you sure about that?" I pointed to Morty. "Morty does have a few red spots on him."

Livvy bit her lip. "He does not."

"Does so," I said. "Maybe they're fish pox."

Livvy looked closer. "Where? I don't see them."

Maxi saw them. "The nurse checked my eyes and said I do have perfect vision with my glasses on." She blinked fast. "TJ, do you have 20/20 vision? You must if you can see the spots."

"Of course I have perfect vision," I joked. "Perfect vision for a perfect kid."

I whispered to Maxi. "Do you see any blue streaks on Morty's tail?"

She shook her head. "I saw them the other day. Maybe my eyesight isn't as good as yours."

Livvy wailed, "You're going to drop him! Give him back."

Maxi handed her the bowl. "I won't drop Morty. Don't worry."

By the time Ms. Perry announced snack was over, I realized two things: 1. Maxi's eyesight was perfect, because the blue streaks on Morty's tail *had* vanished, and 2. Something fishy was going on with Morty.

As I climbed into bed that night, my foot kicked something. I reached under and pulled out a folder. It was Livvy's fish-sitting rules. I had forgotten to bring it back to school. I shoved it on my nightstand and turned out the light.

But I couldn't fall asleep. I kept thinking about Morty. Maybe the icky bowl made him sick the other day. Maybe the dirty water had given him the spots? Good thing I cleaned . . . Oh no!

I shot up in bed and flicked the lamp on. Maybe it wasn't the icky bowl. I skimmed through the pages in the folder until I found it: Change the distilled water in the bowl every other day. Scoop Morty up and put him in a temporary bowl while you scrub the grime away. DO NOT USE SOAP. It will kill Morty.

Distilled water? No soap? Morty wasn't sick. He was dead!

Morty looked different today because he kicked the bucket last night! Livvy must have bought a new fish this morning.

I looked in the mirror. Staring back at me was TJ Trapper, Fish Murderer.

I slid on my slippers and ran to Auntie Stella's room. "Auntie Stella, I have to go see Livvy right now. It's about Morty."

Auntie Stella looked at the clock. "It's nine at night." But when she saw the look on my face, she said, "Get in the car."

Livvy answered the door in her pajamas. "Salutations, TJ. What's wrong?"

I took a deep breath. "I have something to tell you. Something awful. You better sit down."

We sat on her front steps while Auntie Stella went inside.

"I've done something really, really bad," I said. "But it was a mistake. An accident. I swear."

"What happened? It can't be that bad." She lowered her head. "At least not as bad as what I did—twice."

"What did you do?" I asked, hoping her confession would make me feel better.

Livvy started to cry. "I killed Morty."

"No, you didn't, Livvy. *I* killed Morty."

She stood up. "Nope. *I* killed him. He was floating on his back at my house, TJ. I flushed him." She rubbed her eyes. "My mom watched the Fitzpatrick triplets last week. They got carried away with the fish flakes." She chucked a rock across the yard. "I went to Pet Palace and got another fish the next day. You and Maxi noticed it wasn't Morty right away."

"The blue streak on his tail?" I asked.

"The blue streak," said Livvy, nodding. "But then the new one died this morning.

I had to buy another one. I messed up. Big time."

"Not any worse than I did, Livvy. I killed Morty number two. When I was fish-sitting, I cleaned his bowl. I used . . . I used . . . tap water."

Livvy looked shocked.

"And," I continued, "soap."

"Soap!" Livvy shrieked. "You did kill Morty number two. Well, I feel a little better. Bad for Morty but relieved I didn't kill two fish!" She patted my back. "Thanks for telling the truth. I never would have known."

"Should we tell the rest of the class?" I asked.

"No way," said Livvy. "Besides, I found out something interesting at Pet Palace today. Your class had six Taters and two

Tots last year. Every time one died, your teacher replaced it. The store owner said she kept them in business."

It wasn't funny, but I laughed. So did Livvy.

"You know, Livvy. I've been reading up on how to take care of goldfish. The book says that they survive much longer in a filtered tank."

"I should have thought of that. Poppy bought me a filtered tank for my tropical fish. But I didn't think just one fish would need a tank," Livvy said.

"My dad has an old fish tank and filter system somewhere in our attic. If I can find them, would you want to use it?"

"That's a good idea," said Livvy. "A really good idea."

"Maybe you can come over on Friday

night so we can look for it."

Livvy jumped up. "Really? That would be great, TJ."

"My dad says he has some old tents up there, too. If we find one, maybe . . ."

"What?" asked Livvy. "Maybe what?"

I tapped my foot on the second step. "Maybe we can camp out on the first night

of Hanukkah. I'll make you a deal," I said. "I'll bring the s'mores if you bring Morty."

Livvy gave me a high five. "Deal."

The Bully Test

Have you ever been a bully? Ask yourself these questions.

 Do I like to leave others out to make them feel bad?

 Have I ever spread a rumor that I knew was not true?

 Do I like teasing others?

 Do I call others mean names to make myself feel better or get attention?

 Is it funny to me to see other kids getting made fun of?

If you answered yes to any of these questions, it's not too late to change. First, say "I'm sorry." And start treating others the way you want to be treated.

Be a Bully Zapper

A few tips on how to stop bullying that happens around you:

 Report bullying to an adult you trust. This is the most important thing you can do to stop bullying.

 Change the subject when a verbal bully starts bullying his or her target. This may distract him or her from bullying.

 Don't participate in bullying behavior. Even if your friends are being bullies, you can stop the cycle of bullying by not participating.

 Speak up for your friends. Bullies back down if they get attention they don't want.

Bullying Glossary

bystander - someone who watches but is not a part of a situation.

FHO (freezing him/her out) - not talking to someone and excluding him or her from your group.

ignore - to not pay attention to someone or something.

reporting - telling an adult about being bullied.

social bullying - telling secrets, spreading rumors, giving mean looks, and leaving kids out on purpose.

tattling - telling someone about another's actions in order to get him or her in trouble.

upstander - someone who sees bullying and stands up for the person being bullied.

Further Reading

 Fox, Debbie. *Good-Bye Bully Machine.* Minneapolis: Free Spirit Publishing, 2009.

 Hall, Megan Kelley. *Dear Bully: Seventy Authors Tell Their Stories.* New York: HarperTeen, 2011.

 Romain, Trevor. *Bullies Are a Pain in the Brain.* Minneapolis: Free Spirit Publishing, 1997.

Web Sites

To learn more about bullying, visit ABDO Group online. Web sites about bullying are featured on our Book Links page. These links are routinely monitored and updated to provide the most current information available. **www.abdopublishing.com**

About the Author

Lisa Mullarkey is the author of the popular chapter book series, Katharine the Almost Great. She wears many hats: mom, teacher, librarian, and author. She is passionate about children's literature. She lives in New Jersey with her husband, John, and her children, Sarah and Matthew. She's happy to report that none of them are bullies.

About the Illustrator

Gary LaCoste began his illustration career 15 years ago. His clients included Hasbro, Nickelodeon, and Lego. Lately his focus has shifted to children's publishing, where he's enjoyed illustrating more than 25 titles. Gary happily lives in western Massachusetts with his wife, Miranda, and daughter, Ashley.